P9-DVG-648

Illustrated by Christopher Weyant

We Are (Not) Friends

To Andrea, Ilene, Lisa, and Liz.
Thank you for all the fun playdates and belly laughs,
from childhood to adulthood—A. K.

To Tom, for a lifetime of friendship and laughs—C. W.

Published by Two Lions, New York
www.apub.com

ISBN-13: 9781542044288 (hardcover) ISBN-10: 1542044286 (hardcover)
Design by Abby Dening
The illustrations are rendered in ink and watercolor with brush pens on Arches paper.
Printed in China | First edition
1 3 5 7 9 10 8 6 4 2

Can I play with you?

Yes!

Well . . .

Thanks!

BOING BOING

Look!
We can do
a duet.

OK!

But—

TAPPA
TAPPA
TAPPITY
TAPPITY

BONK!

My hat!
WOOOSH
What? It was getting hot.
WHIRRRRRRRR

Let's play
dinosaur
hunters!

Where's
our friend?

Our
friend—

<u>We</u> are friends.

We are *not*
friends with—

I'm back!
BOING
Great! Now we *all* can play dinosaur hunters!
Great.

HEE! HEE! HEE!
HAW! HAW! HAW!

I know!
We can
build
a car!
A
jeep!

Great minds . . .
. . . think alike!

WHAP!
STACK!
STACK!

BEEP!
BEEP!

SQUEAK!
OOOPH!
ERGG!!
Um . . .
it’s a two-seater.
Then where do *I* sit?

You can be the dinosaur!
Yeah! Attack, T. rex!
Roar.

LOUDER!

ROAR!

SCARIER!

ROAR!!!

WHUMP!!!

WE ARE NOT

FRIENDS!!!

SNIFF!

You are right.
We are not friends.
We are *best* friends.

And this is
our *new* friend?

Yay! Do you want to play spies?

Can I
play too?